BC 2/133 General Leander Jefferson 2/18 388.1 818.99

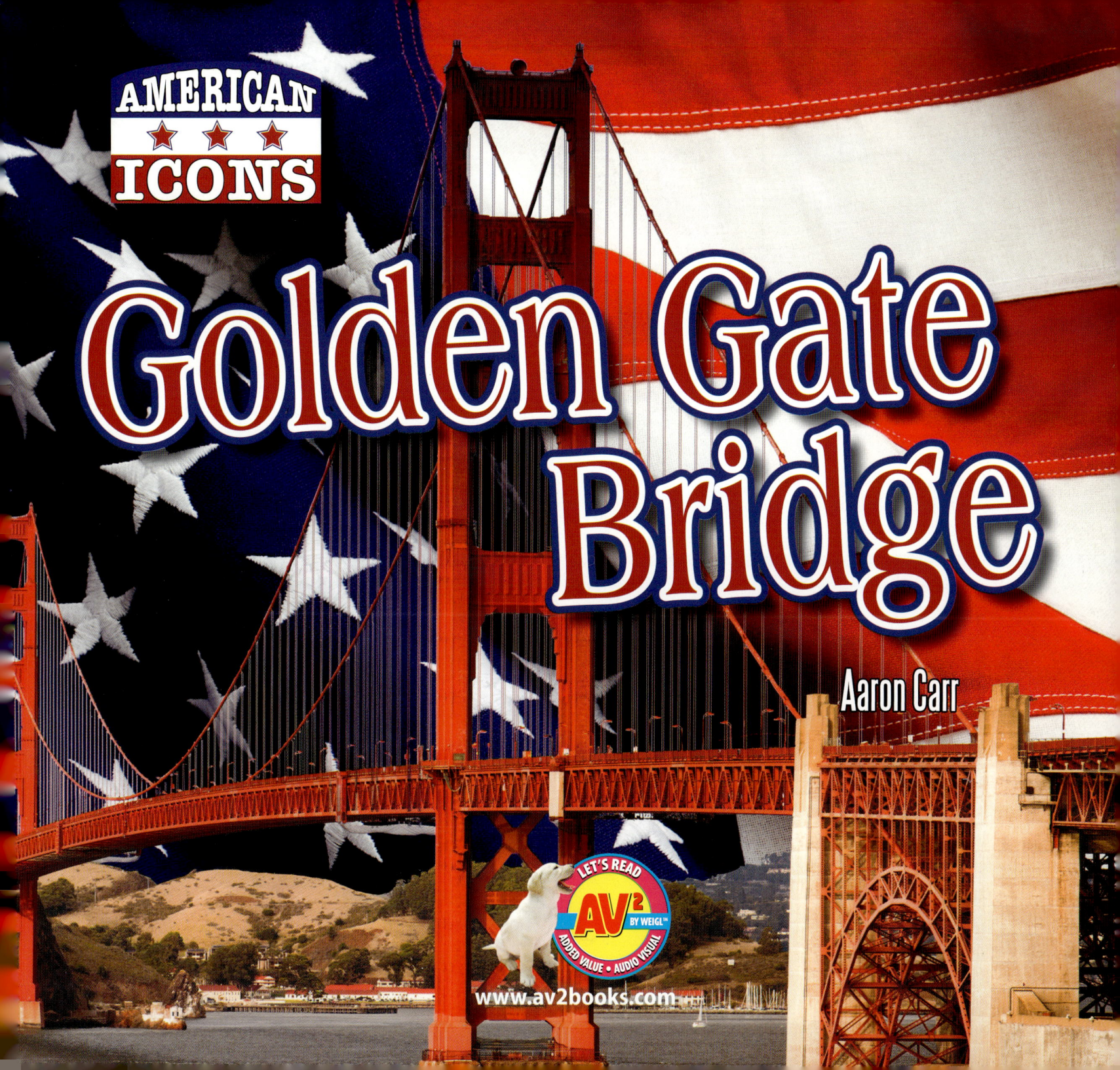

LET'S READ AV² BY WEIGL
ADDED VALUE • AUDIO VISUAL

Go to www.av2books.com, and enter this book's unique code.

BOOK CODE

K733647

AV² by Weigl brings you media enhanced books that support active learning.

AV² provides enriched content that supplements and complements this book. Weigl's AV² books strive to create inspired learning and engage young minds in a total learning experience.

Your AV² Media Enhanced books come alive with...

Audio
Listen to sections of the book read aloud.

Video
Watch informative video clips.

Embedded Weblinks
Gain additional information for research.

Try This!
Complete activities and hands-on experiments.

Key Words
Study vocabulary, and complete a matching word activity.

Quizzes
Test your knowledge.

Slide Show
View images and captions, and prepare a presentation.

... and much, much more!

Published by AV² by Weigl
350 5th Avenue, 59th Floor New York, NY   10118
Websites: www.av2books.com   www.weigl.com

Copyright ©2016 AV² by Weigl
All rights reserved. No part of this publication may be reproduced, stored in a retrieval system, or transmitted in any form or by any means, electronic, mechanical, photocopying, recording, or otherwise, without the prior written permission of the publisher.

Library of Congress Cataloging-in-Publication Data
Carr, Aaron.
 Golden Gate Bridge / Aaron Carr.
     pages cm. -- (American icons)
  ISBN 978-1-4896-2894-7 (hardcover : alk. paper) -- ISBN 978-1-4896-2895-4 (softcover : alk. paper) -- ISBN 978-1-4896-2896-1 (single-user ebk.) -- ISBN 978-1-4896-2897-8 (multi-user ebk.)
 1. Golden Gate Bridge (San Francisco, Calif.)--Juvenile literature. I. Title.
  TG25.S225C47 2014
  388.1'320979461--dc23
                                                            2014038568

Printed in the United States of America in North Mankato, Minnesota
1 2 3 4 5 6 7 8 9 0   18 17 16 15 14

Project Coordinator: Heather Kissock
Designer: Mandy Christiansen

122014
WEP311214

Every reasonable effort has been made to trace ownership and to obtain permission to reprint copyright material. The publishers would be pleased to have any errors or omissions brought to their attention so that they may be corrected in subsequent printings.

Weigl acknowledges Getty Images and iStockphoto as the primary image supplier for this title.

CONTENTS

2 AV² Book Code
4 What Is the Golden Gate Bridge?
6 A National Symbol
8 The Golden Gate
10 Building the Golden Gate Bridge
12 Grand Opening
14 Painting It Orange
16 Keeping the Bridge Safe
18 A Big Event
20 The Golden Gate Bridge Today
22 Golden Gate Bridge Facts
24 Key Words/Log on to www.av2books.com

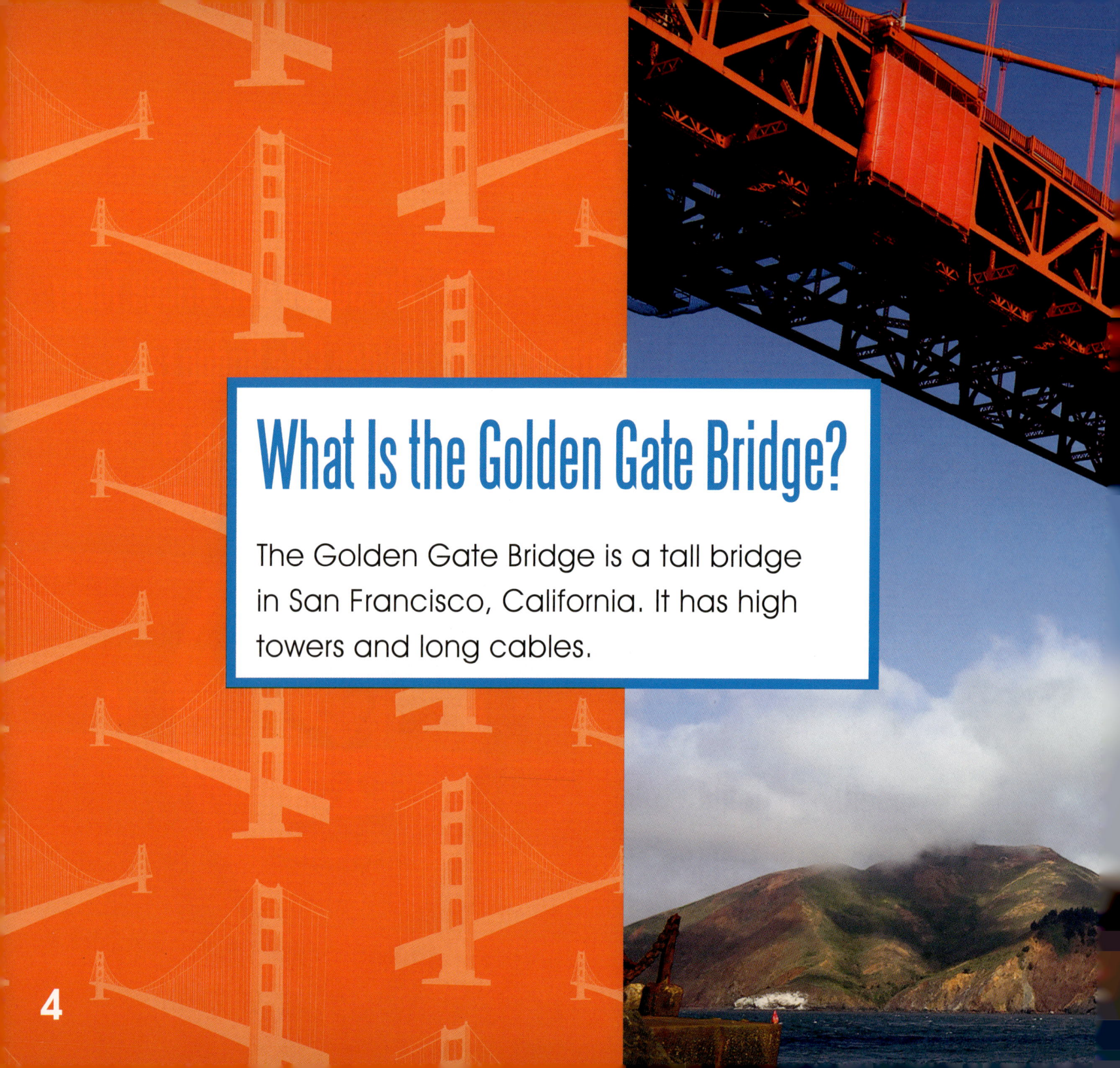

What Is the Golden Gate Bridge?

The Golden Gate Bridge is a tall bridge in San Francisco, California. It has high towers and long cables.

A National Symbol

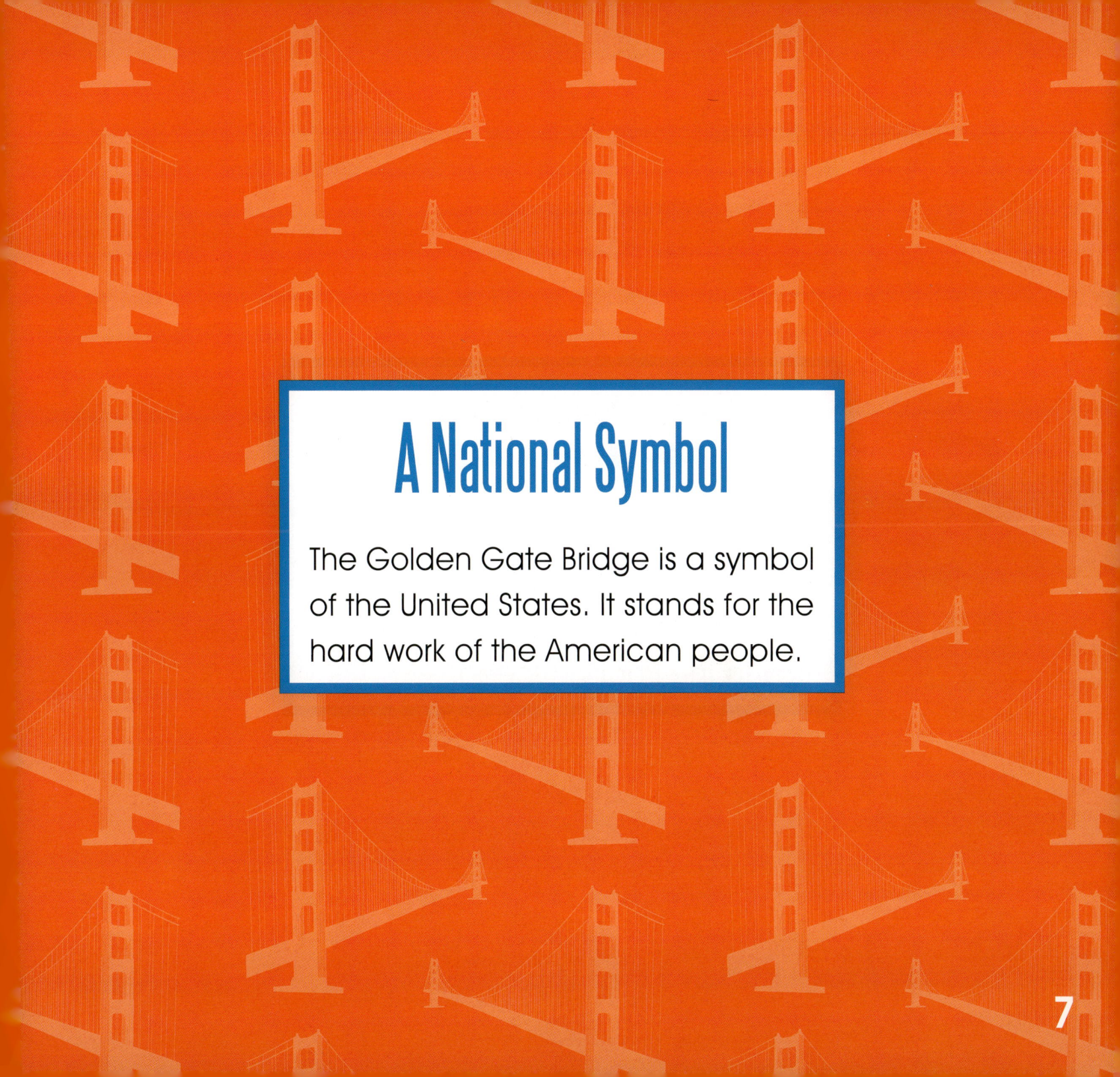

The Golden Gate Bridge is a symbol of the United States. It stands for the hard work of the American people.

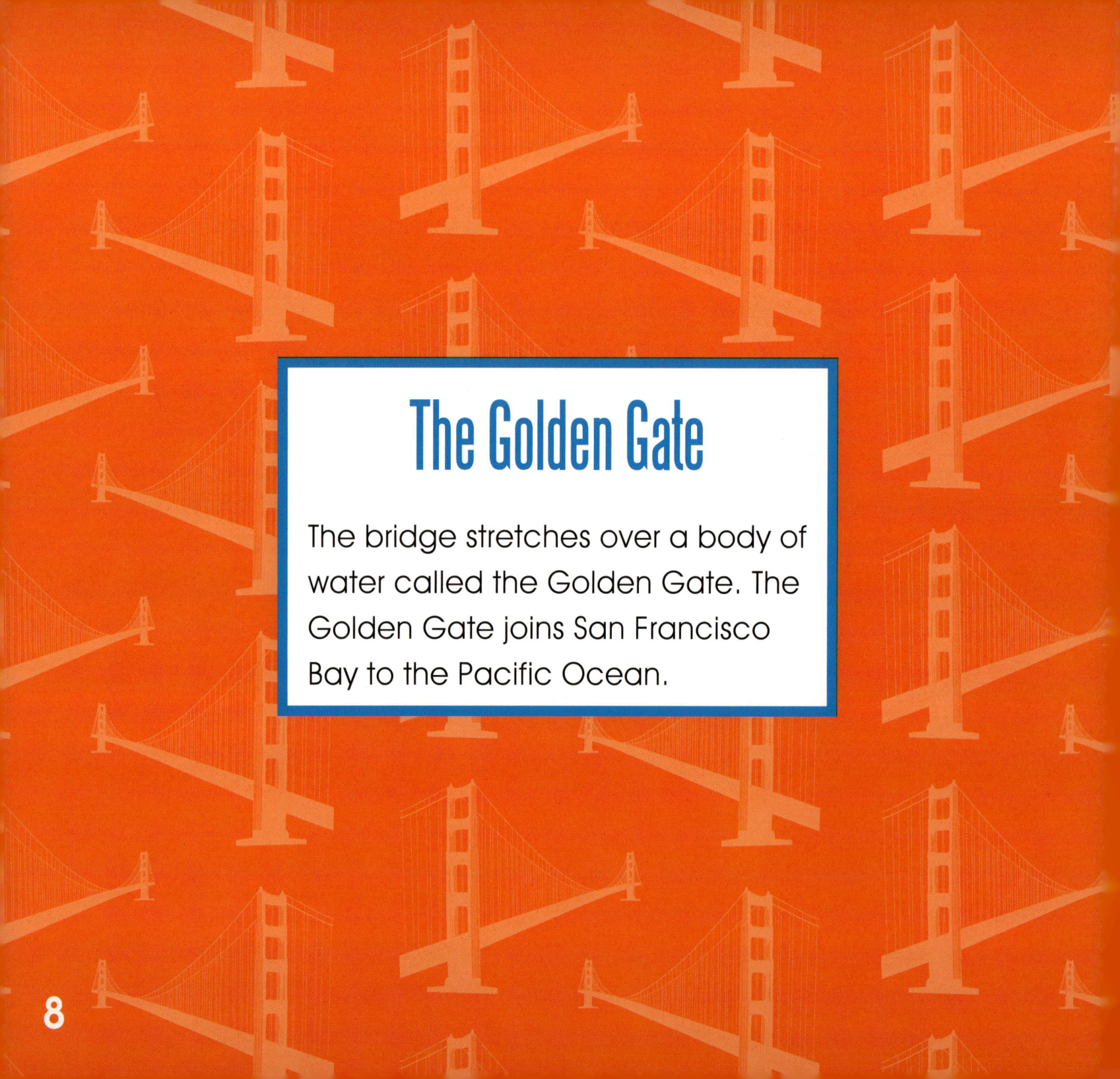

The Golden Gate

The bridge stretches over a body of water called the Golden Gate. The Golden Gate joins San Francisco Bay to the Pacific Ocean.

Building the Golden Gate Bridge

Work on the Golden Gate Bridge started in 1933. It took more than four years to finish the bridge.

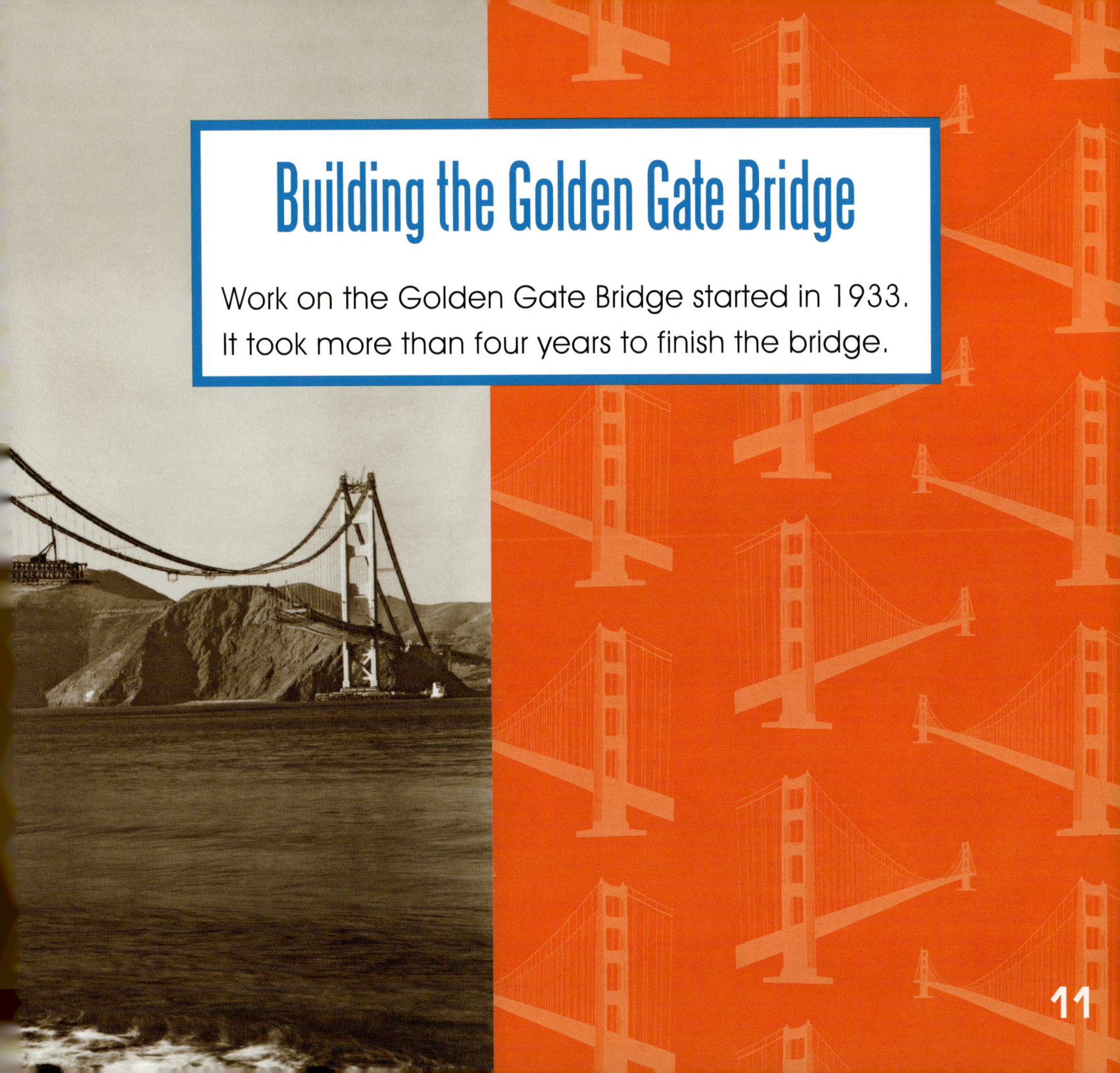

Grand Opening

A special event was held to open the bridge. More than 200,000 people walked across it.

Painting It Orange

The Golden Gate Bridge is painted orange. This bright color helps ships see the bridge from the water.

Keeping the Bridge Safe

People still paint the Golden Gate Bridge. Painting the bridge keeps it safe.

A Big Event

The Golden Gate Bridge turned 75 years old in 2012. A big party was held with music and fireworks.

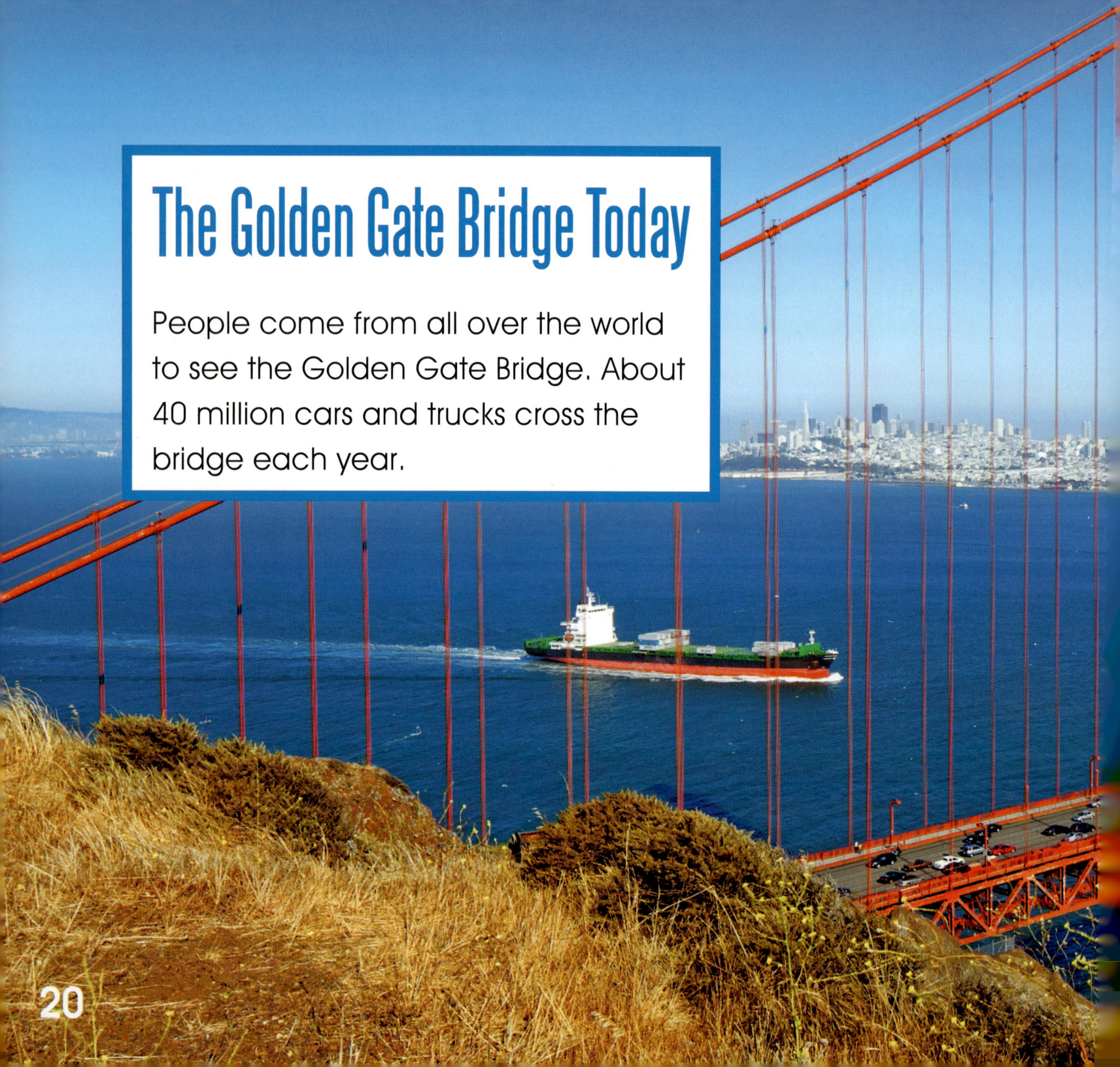

The Golden Gate Bridge Today

People come from all over the world to see the Golden Gate Bridge. About 40 million cars and trucks cross the bridge each year.

GOLDEN GATE BRIDGE FACTS

These pages provide detailed information that expands on the interesting facts found in the book. These pages are intended to be used by adults to help young readers round out their knowledge of each national symbol featured in the *American Icons* series.

Pages 4–5

What Is the Golden Gate Bridge? The Golden Gate Bridge is a suspension bridge that crosses the Golden Gate strait between San Francisco and Marin County, California. The bridge hangs from cables strung over two towers that rise 746 feet (227 meters) above the water. The main span of the bridge, between the towers, is 4,200 feet (1,280 m) long. Until 1964, this was the largest main span of any bridge in the world.

Pages 6–7

A National Symbol The Golden Gate Bridge is known throughout the United States and around the world as a symbol of the American West and of the nation itself. Many people once said that a bridge could not be made to span the Golden Gate. For this reason, the bridge is also seen as a symbol of determination and hard work.

Pages 8–9

The Golden Gate The Golden Gate is a 3-mile (5-kilometer) long strait that forms the northern boundary of San Francisco. All ships traveling to ports in San Francisco Bay or the Sacramento-San Joaquin river system must enter through this gateway. The strait was named by U.S. Army Captain John C. Frémont. The natural gateway reminded Frémont of a harbor in Turkey called the Golden Horn.

Pages 10–11

Building the Golden Gate Bridge Construction of the Golden Gate Bridge began on January 5, 1933. To help with the construction, factories across the country made 83,000 tons (75,296 tonnes) of steel parts and shipped them to San Francisco. There are more than one million steel rivets holding the Golden Gate Bridge together.

Pages 12–13  **Grand Opening** The Golden Gate Bridge held a celebration called Pedestrian Day on May 27, 1937. People were allowed to walk over the bridge before it was opened to vehicle traffic. The next day, a ribbon-cutting ceremony was held, at which point cars began traveling across the strait. Although some people objected to the bridge, the reception after the opening was mostly positive.

Pages 14–15  **Painting It Orange** The Golden Gate Bridge is painted international orange. The color was chosen by architect Irving Morrow. He felt the color matched the warm colors of the landscape while providing a stark contrast to the cool colors of the water and sky. This would make the bridge more visible to ships entering the strait while also maintaining a pleasing appearance.

Pages 16–17  **Keeping the Bridge Safe** Painting is part of the ongoing maintenance of the bridge. The paint protects the bridge from the humidity and saltwater that surround it. It helps to keep the humidity and salt from eating away at the steel. Today, a team of 13 ironworkers, 3 pusher ironworkers, 28 painters, and 5 painter laborers work to maintain the bridge.

Pages 18–19  **A Big Event** On May 24, 1987, the bridge was closed to traffic for five hours to celebrate its 50th anniversary. People flooded onto the bridge to recreate the Pedestrian Day bridge walk of 1937. In 2012, the Golden Gate Festival was held at various places on both sides of the bridge. Events included live music, dance performances, and parades.

Pages 20–21  **The Golden Gate Bridge Today** The Golden Gate Bridge is a heavily used gateway between San Francisco and the suburbs of Marin County. More than 100,000 vehicles cross the bridge each day. Tolls paid to cross the bridge raise more than $100 million per year. The bridge is also a cultural icon, appearing in numerous movies and television shows.

KEY WORDS

Research has shown that as much as 65 percent of all written material published in English is made up of 300 words. These 300 words cannot be taught using pictures or learned by sounding them out. They must be recognized by sight. This book contains 45 common sight words to help young readers improve their reading fluency and comprehension. This book also teaches young readers several important content words, such as nouns. These words are paired with pictures to aid in learning and improve understanding.

Page	Sight Words First Appearance
4	a, and, has, high, in, is, it, long, the, what
7	American, for, hard, of, people, work
8	over, to, water
11	four, more, on, started, than, took, years
13	open, walked, was
14	from, helps, see, this
16	keeps, still
19	big, old, turned, with
20	about, all, cars, come, each, world

Page	Content Words First Appearance
4	cables, California, Golden Gate Bridge, San Francisco, towers
7	symbol, United States
8	bay, body, Golden Gate, Pacific Ocean
13	event
14	color, orange, ships
19	fireworks, music, party
20	trucks

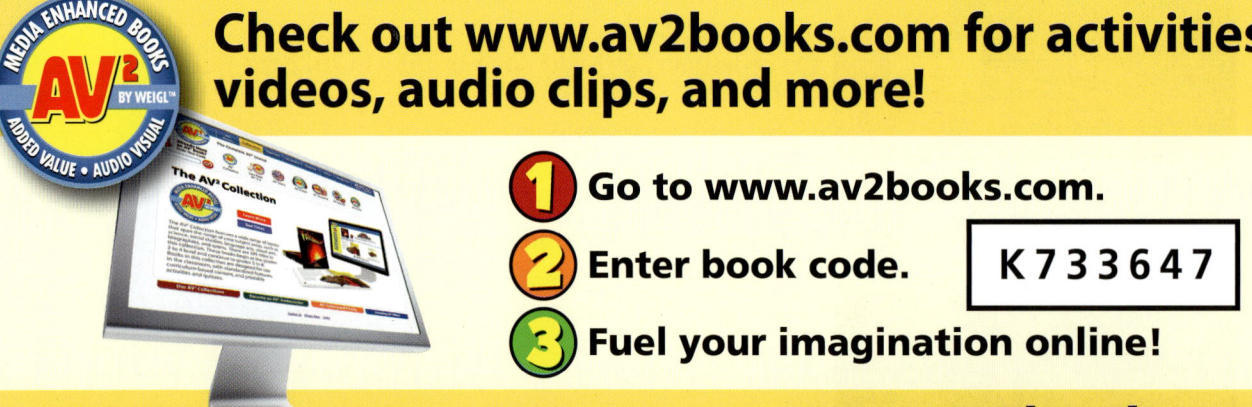

Check out www.av2books.com for activities, videos, audio clips, and more!

1. Go to www.av2books.com.
2. Enter book code. K 7 3 3 6 4 7
3. Fuel your imagination online!

www.av2books.com